Essential
Acoustic
Strumalong

Published 2003
© International Music Publications Limited
Griffin house, 161 Hammersmith Road, London, W6 8BS, England

Editorial, production and recording by Artemis Music Limited
Folio design by Dominic Brookman

How to use this book

All the songs in this book have been carefully arranged to sound great on the acoustic guitar. They all in the same keys as the original recordings, and wherever possible authentic chord voicings ha been used, except in cases where an alternative voicing more accurately reflects the overall tonality

Where a capo was used on the original track, it will be indicated at the top of the song under the ch boxes. If you don't have a capo, you can still play the song, but it won't sound in the same key as backing track. Where a song is played in an altered tuning, that is also indicated at the top of the so

Understanding chord boxes

Chord boxes show the neck of your guitar as if viewed head on – the vertical lines represent the strings (low E to high E, from left to right), and the horizontal lines represent the frets.

An x above a string means 'don't play this string'.

A o above a string means 'play this open string'.

The black dots show you where to put your fingers.

A curved line joining two dots on the fr board represents a 'barre'. This mea that you flatten one of your fretti fingers (usually the first) so that y hold down all the strings between t two dots, at the fret marked.

A fret marking at the side of the chord b shows you where chords that are play higher up the neck are located.

E

7fr.

Tuning your guitar

On Track 1 of the CD you'll find a set of tuning notes. Each string is played in turn, from the bottom E string up to the top E string. Make sure that you tune your guitar to these reference tones carefully, otherwise you won't be in tune with the backing tracks. Alternatively, use an electronic tuner.

Track 1

Tuning note

How to use the CD

On the CD you'll find soundalike backing tracks for each song in the book. The vocal parts have b omitted, so that you can sing along if you want to.

Each track is preceded by a two-bar count-in, to give you the tempo of the song.

Contents

All You Good Good People

Words and Music by
DANIEL McNAMARA AND RICHARD McNAMARA

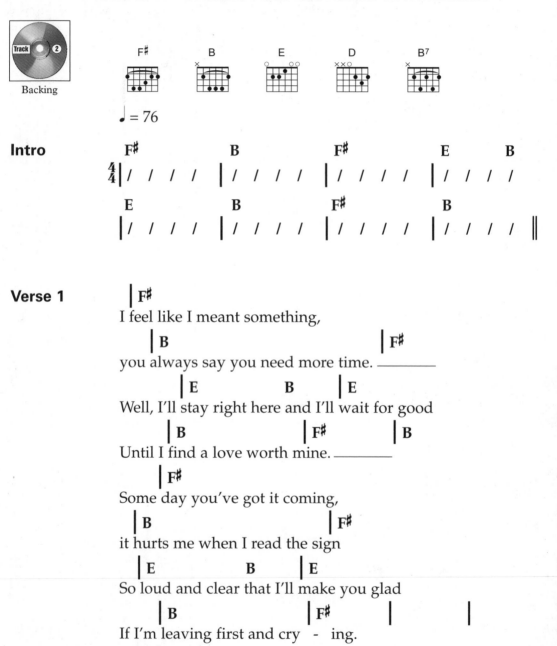

Track 2 — Backing

Chords: F# B E D B7

♩ = 76

Intro

|: F# | B | F# | E   B |

| E | B | F# | B   :||

Verse 1

| F#
I feel like I meant something,

| B | F#
you always say you need more time. _____

| E   B | E
Well, I'll stay right here and I'll wait for good

| B | F# | B
Until I find a love worth mine. _____

| F#
Some day you've got it coming,

| B | F#
it hurts me when I read the sign

| E   B | E
So loud and clear that I'll make you glad

| B | F# | |
If I'm leaving first and cry - ing.

Chorus 1

| E | | B | F# |

All you good, good people listen to me: _____

| | | E |

You're just about done with the way that you feel.

| B | | F# |

There's nothing rings home enough to dig your heels in. _____

| | | E |

You don't have to leave me to see what I mean.

| B | F# | B | |

All you good, good people listen to me.

Link

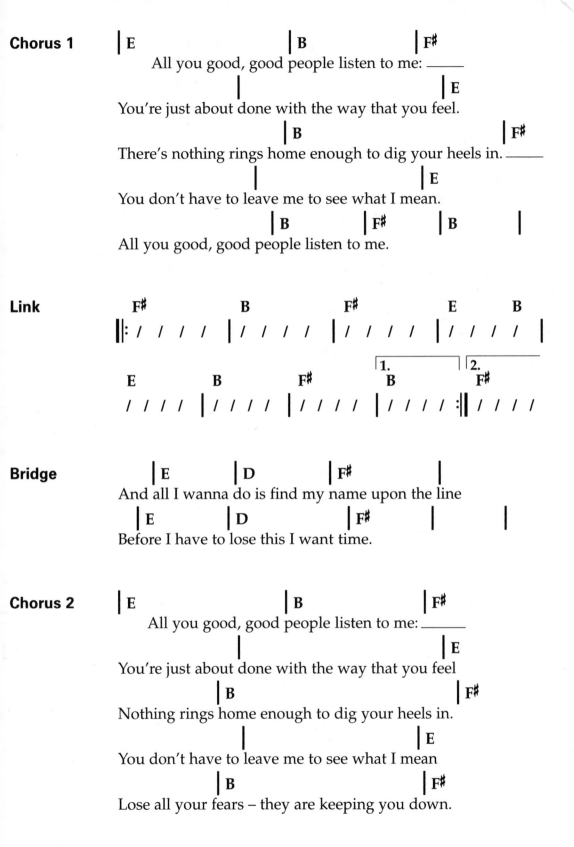

F#   B   F#   E   B

‖: / / / / | / / / / | / / / / | / / / / |

1.   2.

E   B   F#   B   F#

/ / / / | / / / / | / / / / | / / / / :‖ / / / /

Bridge

| E | D | F# | |

And all I wanna do is find my name upon the line

| E | D | F# | | |

Before I have to lose this I want time.

Chorus 2

| E | | B | F# |

All you good, good people listen to me: _____

| | | E |

You're just about done with the way that you feel

| B | | F# |

Nothing rings home enough to dig your heels in.

| | | E |

You don't have to leave me to see what I mean

| B | | F# |

Lose all your fears – they are keeping you down.

| | E

You won't have to fake it while I'm around.

                        | B | F♯ | B⁷

All you good, good people listen to me.

Coda

| F♯   B⁷   F♯   B⁷   *Play 3 times*

‖: / / / / | / / / / | / / / / | / / / / :‖

| B⁷

/ / / / | / / / / | / / / / | / / / / |

‖: F♯ | B⁷

Listen to me,

         | F♯

Listen to me,

         | B⁷   :‖ *Play 3 times*

Listen to me.

| F♯   B⁷   F♯   B⁷   *Play 4 times*

‖: / / / / | / / / / | / / / / | / / / / :‖

| F♯

/ / / / | / / / / | / / / / ‖

6

American English

Words and Music by
COLIN NEWTON, RODDY WOOMBLE,
ROD PRYCE-JONES AND BOB FAIRFOULL

G   Em   Cmaj7

D   C   Dsus4

♩ = 112   **Capo 4th fret**

Intro

G

$\frac{4}{4}$ | / / / / | / / / / | / / / / |

Verse 1

| G | | Em | |

Songs, when the truth are all dedicated to you. In this in-

| Cmaj7 | | G | |

-visible world I choose to live in. And if you be-

| G | | Em | |

-lieve that then now I understand why words mean so much to

| Cmaj7 | | G | |

you. They'll never be about you. Maybe you're

Verse 2

| G | | |

young without youth, or maybe you're

| Em | | |

old without knowing anything's

| Cmaj7 | | G | |

true. I think you're young without youth. Then

Pre-Chorus
| D | C | |
you contract the American dream, you
| Em | D | |
never look up once.
| D | C | |
You've contracted American dreams.
| Em | D | |
I require you to stop and look up.

Chorus
| G | D | Em | C |
Sing a song about myself, keep singing a song about myself.
| G | D | Em | C |
Not some invisible world.

Verse 3
| G | | |
Constantly searching to find something new,   but
| Em | | |
what will you find when you think that nothing's
| Cmaj7 | | G |
true?   Maybe it's that nothing is new.   So you let me hear
| G | Em | |
songs that were written all about you. The good
| | Cmaj7 | |
songs weren't written for   you.   They'll
| | G | | |
never be about you.   And

Pre-Chorus
| D | C | |
you contract the American dream, you
| Em | D | |
never look up once.
| D | C | |
You've contracted American dreams, you'll
| Em | D | |
never look up once, so don't look up.

Chorus

G	D	Em	C	

Sing a song about myself, keep singing a song about myself.

G	D	Em	C	

Not some invisible world.

G	D	Em	C	

Sing a song about myself, keep singing a song about myself.

G	D	Em	C	

Not some invisible world.   And I won't

Bridge

D	Em	G	C	

tell you what this means, 'cos you already know. And I won't

D	Em	G	C		

tell you what this means, 'cos you already know.   So

Chorus

G	D	Em	C	

Sing a song about myself, keep singing a song about myself.

G	D	Em	C	

Not some invisible world.   And you

G	D	

came along and found the

Em	C

weak heart that you've always wanted.

G	D	Em	C	

And let yourself be everything that you've always wanted.

G	D	Em	C	

It doesn't have to be so decided   that you've always wanted.

G	D	Em	C	

And no need for explanations   you've always wanted.

Outro

G	Dsus4	Em	C

And you'll find what you find when you find there's nothing.

G	Dsus4	Em	C	G

And you'll find what you find when you find there's nothing.

The Drugs Don't Work

Words and Music by
RICHARD ASHCROFT

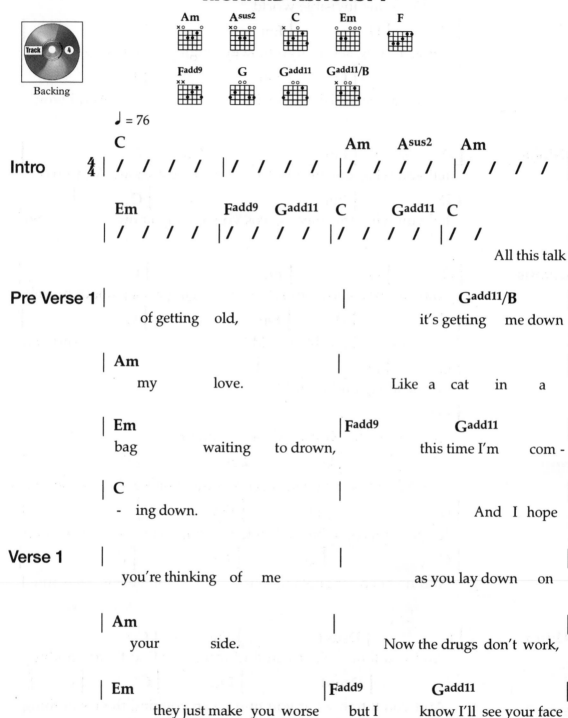

```
          | C                  Gadd11        | C                                              |
            again.                             Now the drugs  don't  work,

Chorus 1  | Em                              |Fadd9         G                              |
              they just make  you  worse       but I       know I'll see your face

          | C                  Gadd11        | C                                              |
            again.                                                   But   I  know

Verse 2   |                                 |                                              |
              I'm on    a losing    streak,               as   I  pass down my

          | Am                              |                                              |
              old          street.                     And  if  you   want    to

          | Em                              |Fadd9           Gadd11                      |
            show        just let   me   know      and I'll    sing  in your  ear

          | C                  Gadd11        | C                                              |
            again.                             Now the drugs  don't  work,

Chorus 2  | Em                              |Fadd9         G                              |
              they just make  you  worse       but I       know I'll see your face

          | C                  Gadd11        |                                              |
            again.                                          Coz baby

Bridge 1  | F                               | Em                                           |
            ooh,                                           if    heaven    calls

          | Am                              |Gadd11  G                                   |
                I'm   coming     too.              Just like you       say,

          | F                               | Em                                           |
                                                            you'll leave my life,

          | Am                              | Gadd11                                      |
              I'm  better   off dead.                      All this talk

Verse 3   | C                               |                                              |
              of getting old,                              it's  getting me down
```

| Am | |

     my   love.   Like a cat in a

| Em | Fadd9   Gadd11 |

bag   waiting   to drown,   this time I'm   com -

| C   Gadd11 | C |

- ing down.   Now the drugs don't work,

Chorus 3 | Em | Fadd9   G |

they just make you worse   but I   know I'll see your face

| C   Gadd11 | |

again.   Coz baby

Bridge 2 | F | Em |

ooh,   if heaven calls

| Am | Gadd11 G |

I'm coming   too.   Just like you   say,

| F | Em |

you'll leave my life,

| Am | Gadd11 |

I'm better off dead.   But if you want a

| Em | F   Gadd11 |

show,   then just let me know and I'll sing in your ear

| C | |

again.   Now the drugs don't work,

Chorus 4 | Em | F   G |

they just make you worse   but I   know I'll see your face

| C   Gadd11 | C   Gadd11 |

again,   yeah I know I'll see your face

| C   Gadd11 | C   Gadd11 |

again,   yeah I know I'll see your face

(Repeat last 2 bars to end)

Grace

Words and Music by
DANIEL GOFFEY, GARETH COOMBES,
MICHAEL QUINN AND ROBERT COOMBES

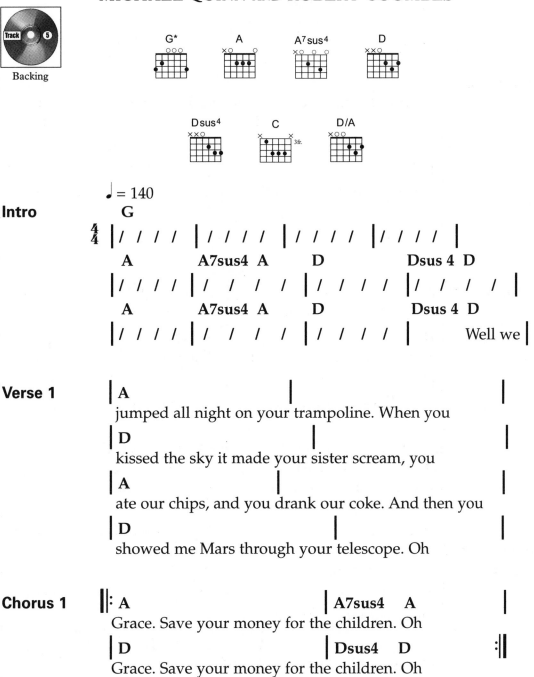

♩ = 140

Intro

G
| / / / / | / / / / | / / / / | / / / / |

A   A7sus4 A   D   Dsus 4 D
| / / / / | / / / / | / / / / | / / / / |

A   A7sus4 A   D   Dsus 4 D
| / / / / | / / / / | / / / / | Well we |

Verse 1

| A | |
jumped all night on your trampoline. When you

| D | |
kissed the sky it made your sister scream, you

| A | |
ate our chips, and you drank our coke. And then you

| D | |
showed me Mars through your telescope. Oh

Chorus 1

||: A | A7sus4   A |
Grace. Save your money for the children. Oh

| D | Dsus4   D | :||
Grace. Save your money for the children. Oh

|G | |
Grace. Save your money for the children. Oh
|A | |
Grace. Save your money   save your money. Go!
  D   C   G   D/A
| / / / / | Well you |

Verse 2 |D | |
              sang your songs and you made us laugh. So we
              |A | |
              captured you in a   photograph, and when the
              |D | |
              stars came out, your mother called your name, but when the
              |A | |
              morning comes, we'll be together again. Oh

Chorus 1   ‖: A |A7sus4   A |
               Grace. Save your money for the children. Oh
               |D |Dsus4   D   :‖
               Grace. Save your money for the children. Oh
               |G | |
               Grace. Save your money for the children. Oh
               |A | |
               Grace. Save your money   save your money. Go!
                 D   C   G   D/A
               | / / / / | / / / / |

Bridge |D | / / / / |
              Save your money.
              |A | / / / / |
              Save your money for the...
              |D | |
              Save your money for the children.

14

```
    |A              |              |
    Save your money for the children.
    C                      G
    | / / / / | / / / / | / / / / | / / / / |
```

Link
```
        A           A7sus4  A       D           Dsus 4  D
    | / / / / | /  /  /  / | /  /  /  / | /  /  /  / |
        A           A7sus4  A       D           Dsus 4  D
    | / / / / | /  /  /  / | / / / / |          Oh   |
```

Chorus 1
```
    |G                      |                      |
    Grace. Save your money for the children. Oh
    |A                      |                      |
    Grace. Save your money       save your money. Go!
    D    C    G   D/A
    | / / / / | / / / / |
    D    C    G   D
    | / / / / | / / / / ‖
```

Handbags And Gladrags

Words and Music by
MIKE D'ABO

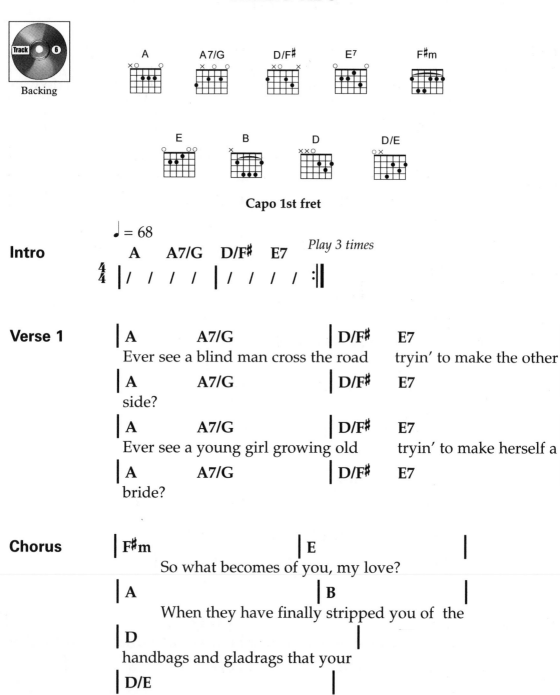

Capo 1st fret

Intro

♩ = 68

A   A7/G   D/F♯   E7   *Play 3 times*

$\frac{4}{4}$ | / / / / | / / / / :||

Verse 1

| A   A7/G | D/F♯   E7 |
Ever see a blind man cross the road   tryin' to make the other

| A   A7/G | D/F♯   E7 |
side?

| A   A7/G | D/F♯   E7 |
Ever see a young girl growing old   tryin' to make herself a

| A   A7/G | D/F♯   E7 |
bride?

Chorus

| F♯m | E |
So what becomes of you, my love?

| A | B |
When they have finally stripped you of the

| D |
handbags and gladrags that your

| D/E |
poor old grand-dad had to sweat to buy

Link

```
|A          A7/G            D/F#    E7
    you.                  |  /  /  /  /  |

 A    A7/G   D/F#   E7
|  /  /  /  /  |  /  /  /  /  |
```

Verse 2

```
|A                  A7/G    |D/F#                 E7              |
    Once I was a young man   and all I thought I had to do was
|A          A7/G            |D/F#    E7                           |
 smile.
|A                  A7/G    |D/F#      E7                          |
   Well you are still a young girl   and you bought everything in
|A          A7/G            |D/F#    E7                           |
 style.
```

Chorus

```
|F#m                        |E                      |
     So once you think you're in, you're out
|A                          |B                      |
        'cos you don't mean a single thing without the
|D                          |
 handbags and gladrags that your
|D/E                        |
 poor old grand-dad had to sweat to buy
```

Link

```
|A          A7/G            D/F#    E7
    you.                  |  /  /  /  /  |

 A    A7/G   D/F#   D/E    A    D/E
|  /  /  /  /  |  /  /  /  /  |  /  /  /  /  |
```

Verse 3

```
|A                  A7/G    |D/F#  E7                             |
 Sing a song of sixpence for his sake   and drink a bottle full of
|A          A7/G            |D/F#    E7                           |
 rye.
```

```
|A              A7/G        |D/F♯      E7              |
Four and twenty blackbirds in a cake. And bake them all in a
|A          A7/G            |D/F♯    E7          |
pie.
```

Chorus
```
|F♯m                        |E                  |
They told me you missed school today
|A                          |B                  |
So what I suggest, you just throw them all away. The
|D                          |
handbags and gladrags that your
|D/E                        |
poor old grand-dad had to sweat to buy.
```

Link

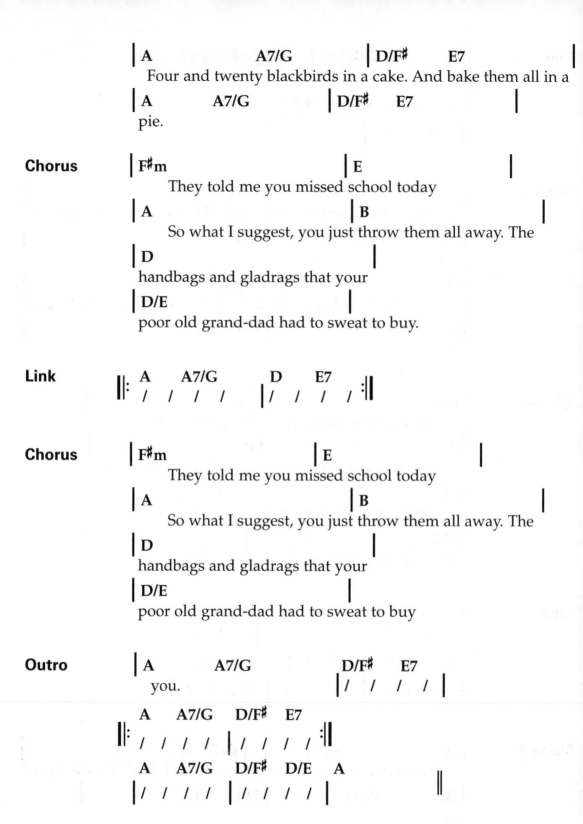

```
        A    A7/G        D     E7
     ‖: /  /  /  /    | /  /  /  / :‖
```

Chorus
```
|F♯m                        |E                  |
They told me you missed school today
|A                          |B                  |
So what I suggest, you just throw them all away. The
|D                          |
handbags and gladrags that your
|D/E                        |
poor old grand-dad had to sweat to buy
```

Outro
```
|A          A7/G            D/F♯    E7
  you.                    | /  /  /  / |

     A    A7/G   D/F♯   E7
  ‖: /  /  /  / | /  /  /  / :‖

     A    A7/G   D/F♯   D/E   A
  | /  /  /  / | /  /  /  / |          ‖
```

18

Hotel Yorba

Words and Music by
JACK WHITE

Backing

♩ = 97

Intro

G

4/4 | / / / / | / / / |

Verse 1

|G
I was watching

|C
With one eye on the other side,

|D
I had 15 people telling me to move,

|G
I got moving on my mind.

|
I found shelter

|C
In some thoughts turning wheels around.

|D
I said thirty-nine times that I love you

|G
To the beauty I have found.

Chorus 1

|G
Well, it's one, two, three, four, take the elevator

```
                     | C
At the Hotel Yorba I'll be glad to see ya later
| D                              | G     F     G              |
      All they got inside is vacancy.      /     /     /
```

Link 1
```
          G             C             D             G
| /  /  /  /  | /  /  /  /  | /  /  /  /  | /  /  /
```

Verse 2
```
                | G
I've been thinking
                | C
Of a little place down by the lake:
                | D
They got a dirty, old road

Leading up to the house
                | G
I wonder how long it will take

                |
'Til we're alone?
                    | C
Sitting on the front porch of that home,
| D
Stomping our feet on the wooden boards;
          | G
We never got to worry about  locking the door.
```

Chorus 2
```
                    | G
Well, it's one, two, three, four, take the elevator
          | C
At the Hotel Yorba I'll be glad to see ya later
| D                              | G     F     G              |
      All they got inside is vacancy.      /     /     /
```

Link 2

G	C	D	G
/ / / /	/ / / /	/ / / /	/ / /

Verse 3

|G
It might sound silly

|C
For me to think childish thoughts like these

|D
But I'm so tired of acting tough

|G
And I'm gonna do what I please.

|
Let's get married

|C
In a big cathedral by a priest,

|D
'Cause if I'm the man that you love the most

|G
You can say 'I do' at least.

Chorus 3

|G
Well, it's one, two, three, four, take the elevator

|C
At the Hotel Yorba I'll be glad to see ya later

|D |G
　　All they got inside is vacancy.

Chorus 4

|G
And it's four, five, six, seven, grab your umbrella,

|C
Grab a hold of me 'cause I'm your favourite fella,

|D |G   C   G D G ‖
　　All they got inside is vacancy.

Karma Police

Words and Music by
THOMAS YORKE, JONATHAN GREENWOOD,
PHILIP SELWAY, COLIN GREENWOOD
AND EDWARD O'BRIEN

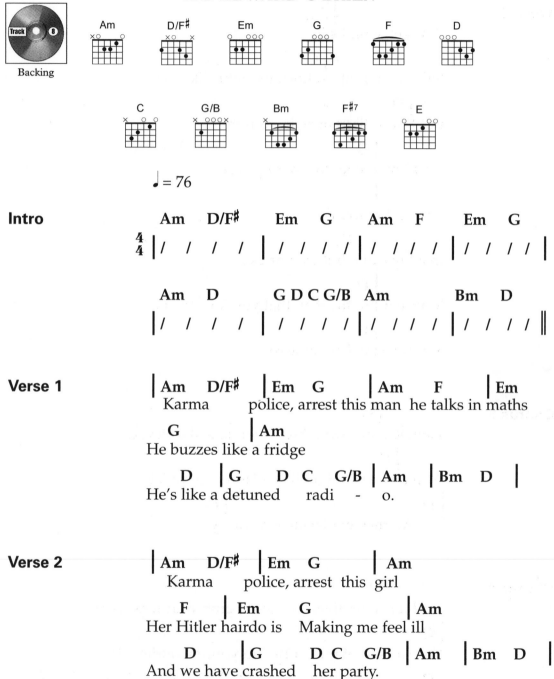

Track 8 — Backing

Chords: Am D/F# Em G F D C G/B Bm F#7 E

♩ = 76

Intro

| Am D/F# | Em G | Am F | Em G |
|/ / / / |/ / / / |/ / / / |/ / / / |

| Am D | G D C G/B | Am | Bm D |
|/ / / / |/ / / / |/ / / / |/ / / / |

Verse 1

|Am D/F# |Em G |Am F |Em
Karma   police, arrest this man he talks in maths

G |Am
He buzzes like a fridge

D |G D C G/B |Am |Bm D |
He's like a detuned   radi - o.

Verse 2

|Am D/F# |Em G |Am
Karma   police, arrest this girl

F |Em G |Am
Her Hitler hairdo is Making me feel ill

D |G D C G/B |Am |Bm D |
And we have crashed her party.

Bridge 1

|C   D |G F#7 |C   D |G F#7 |
This is what you get   This is what you get

|C   D |G   Bm |C |Bm D |
This is what you get when you mess with us.

Verse 3

|Am D/F# |Em   G |Am
Karma   Police I've given all I can

F |Em   G |Am
It's not enough I've given all I can

D |G   D C   G/B |Am |Bm D |
But we're still on the   payroll.

Bridge 2

|C   D |G F#7 |C   D |G   F#7 |
This is what you get   This is what you get

|C   D |G   Bm |C |Bm D |
This is what you get when you mess with us.

Outro

|Bm   D |G   D/F# |G   D/F# | E
And for a minute there, I lost myself, I lost myself

|Bm   D |G   D/F# |G   D/F# | E
And for a minute there, I lost myself, I lost myself.

Bm   D   G   D/F#   G   D/F#   E
| /   /   /   / | / / / / | / / / | / / / / |

|Bm   D |G   D/F# |G   D/F# | E
For for a minute there, I lost myself, I lost myself

|Bm   D |G   D/F# |G   D/F# | E
Phew, for a minute there, I lost myself, I lost myself.

||: Bm D   G   D/F#
   / / / / | / / / / |

G   D/F#   E   Bm
| / / / / | / / / / / :|| / ||

Love Burns

Words and Music by
PETER HAYES, ROBERT BEEN
AND NICHOLAS JAGO

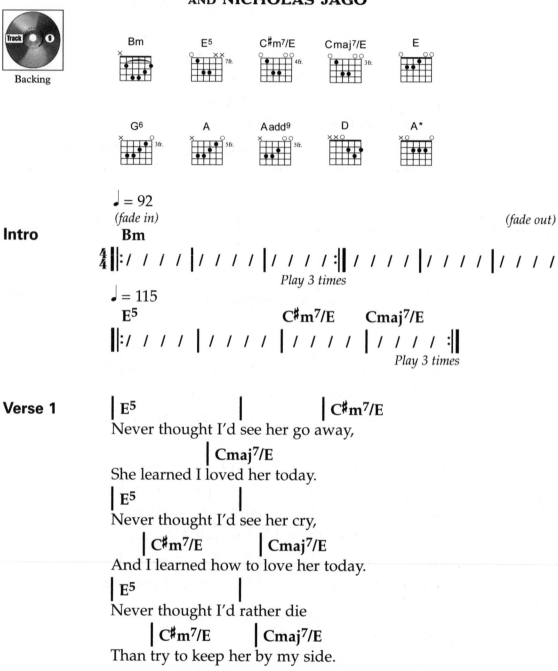

Intro

$\bullet$ = 92
(fade in)

Bm

(fade out)

$\frac{4}{4}$ ‖: / / / / | / / / / | / / / / :‖ / / / / | / / / / | / / / /

Play 3 times

$\bullet$ = 115

E⁵   **C♯m⁷/E**   **Cmaj⁷/E**

‖: / / / / | / / / / | / / / / | / / / / :‖

Play 3 times

Verse 1

| **E⁵** | | **C♯m⁷/E**
Never thought I'd see her go away,

| **Cmaj⁷/E**
She learned I loved her today.

| **E⁵** |
Never thought I'd see her cry,

| **C♯m⁷/E** | **Cmaj⁷/E**
And I learned how to love her today.

| **E⁵** |
Never thought I'd rather die

| **C♯m⁷/E** | **Cmaj⁷/E**
Than try to keep her by my side.

Chorus 1   ‖: E   G⁶ |A   G⁶   :‖ *Play 3 times*

Now she's gone love burns inside me.

Link   E⁵   C♯m⁷/E   Cmaj⁷/E

| / / / / | / / / / | /   / / / | /   / / / |

Verse 2 | E⁵ |

Nothing else can hurt us now,

| C♯m⁷/E | Cmaj⁷/E

No loss, our love's been hung on a cross.

| E⁵ |

Nothing seems to make a sound,

| C♯m⁷/E | Cmaj⁷/E

And now it's all so clear somehow.

| E⁵ |

Nothing really matters now,

| C♯m⁷/E | Cmaj⁷/E

We're gone and on our way.

Chorus 2   ‖: E   G⁶ |A   G⁶   :‖ *Play 3 times*

Now she's gone love burns inside me.

Bridge | E | G⁶

She cuts my skin and bruise my lips,

| Aadd⁹ |

She's   everything to me. ———

| E | G⁶

She tears my clothes and burns my eyes,

| Aadd⁹ |

She's   all I want to see.

| E | G⁶

She brings the cold and scars my soul,

| **Aadd⁹** | |

She's　　　heaven sent to me.

Chorus 3　　‖: E　　　　G⁶ | A　　　　G⁶　　:‖ *Play 3 times*

Now she's gone love burns inside me.

Coda　| E　　　　　　G⁶　　　　　| A　　　G⁶

Never thought I'd need you like the way that I do, yeah.

　　　| E　　G⁶　　| A　　　G⁶

With a kiss, my love, and a wish you're gone.

　　　| E　　G⁶　　| A　　　G⁶

With a kiss my love and a wish you're gone.

| E　　　　　　G⁶　　　　　| A　　　G⁶

Never thought I'd need you like the way that I do.

　　　| E　　G⁶　　| A　　　G⁶

With a kiss, my love, and a wish you're gone.

　　　| E　　G⁶　　| A　　　G⁶

With a kiss, my love, and a wish you're gone.

Play 3 times

Chorus 4　　‖: E　　　　G⁶ | A　　　　G⁶　:‖

Now she's gone love burns inside me.

♩ = 134

　　　E　　　　　　E　　D　A*

6/4 | / / / / / / 4/4 | / / / / |

Coda　　　E　　　D　A*

5/4 ‖: / / / / / :‖ *Repeat to fade*

26

Poor Misguided Fool

Words and Music by
JAMES WALSH, JAMES STELFOX,
BARRY WESTHEAD AND BENJAMIN BYRNE

Track 10

Backing

Am   Em   E7   F

G   C   G/B

♩ = 117   Capo 4th fret

Intro

Am

4/4 ‖: / / / / | / / / / :‖

Verse 1

| Am | | Em | |

Soon as you sound like him,   give me a call.

| E7 | | Am | |

When you're so sensitive,   it's a long way to fall.

| Am | | Em | |

Whenever you need a home,   I will be there.

| E7 | | Am | |

Whenever you're all alone,   and nobody cares.

Chorus 1

| Am | | Em | |

You're just a poor misguided fool

| E7 | | Am | |

Who thinks they know what I should do.

| Am | | Em | |

Life for me and life for you.

| E7 | | Am | |

I lose my right to a point of view.

Verse 2

Am		Em		

Whenever you reach for me,   I'll be your guide.

E7		Am		

Whenever you need someone   so keep it inside.

Am		Em		

Whenever you need a home,   I will be there.

E7		Am		

Whenever you're all alone,   and nobody cares.

Chorus 2

Am		Em		

You're just a poor misguided fool

E7		Am		

Who thinks they know what I should do.

Am		Em		

Life for me and life for you.

E7		Am		

I lose my right to a point of view.

Bridge

F		G		C	G/B	Am	

I'll be your guide   in the morn   ing.

F		G		E7		

You'll cover up bullet-holes.

Link

Am   Em

/ / / /	/ / / /	/ / / /	/ / / /

E7   Am

/ / / /	/ / / /	/ / / /	/ / / /

Verse 3

Am		Em		

Soon as you sound like him,   give me a call.

E7		Am		

When you're so sensitive,   it's a long way to fall.

Chorus 3

| Am | | | Em | | |

You're just a poor misguided fool

| E7 | | | Am | | |

Who thinks they know what I should do.

| Am | | | Em | | |

Life for me and life for you.

| E7 | | | Am | | |

I lose my right to a point of view.

| Am | ‖

Powder Blue

Words and Music by
GUY GARVEY, MARK POTTER,
CRAIG POTTER, RICHARD JUPP
AND PETE TURNER

Backing

C   Cmaj7   Em   G   G/F#   G/F   E7

Capo 3rd fret

$\downarrow$ = 63

Intro

C   Cmaj7   Em

4/4 ‖: / / / / | / / / / | / / / / | / / / / :‖

Verse 1

| C

Your eyes are just like black spiders,

| Cmaj7 | Em

Your hair and dress in ribbons.

|

Babycakes.

| C | Cmaj7

In despair or incoherent, nothing in between.

| Em

China white, my bride tonight

|

Smiling on the tiles.

Chorus 1

| G | G/F#

Bring that minute back

| G/F

We never get so close as when

| E7

The sunward flight begins.

Warner/Chappell Music Publishing Ltd, London W6 8BS

|G |G/F#
I share it all with you
        |G/F |E⁷ | |
Powder blue. _____

Verse 2 |C
          Stumble through the crowds together.
|Cmaj⁷ |Em
       They're trying to ignore us –

|
That's okay.
    |C
I'm proud to be the one you hold
|Cmaj⁷
When the shakes begin
|Em
Sallow-skinned, starry-eyed,

|
Blessed in our sin.

Chorus 2 |G |G/F#
       Bring that minute back –
          |G/F
We never get so close to death.
          |E⁷
Makes you so alive.
   |G |G/F#
I share it all with you,
     |G/F |E⁷ | | | |
Powder blue. _____   hey, yeah. _____

Instrumental   C   Cmaj⁷   Em

‖: / / / / | /   / / / | / / / / | / / / / :‖

Chorus 3 |G |G/F$\sharp$

Bring that minute back

|G/F

We never get so close as when

|E^7

The sunward flight begins.

|G |G/F$\sharp$

I share it all with you

|G/F |E^7 |E | | |

Powder blue. _____

Coda   C   Cmaj^7 Em

| / / / / | /   / / / | / / / / | / / / / |

         C   Cmaj^7 Em

| / / / / | /   / / / | / / / / ‖

There Goes The Fear

Words and Music by
JIMI GOODWIN, JEZ WILLIAMS AND ANDY WILLIAMS

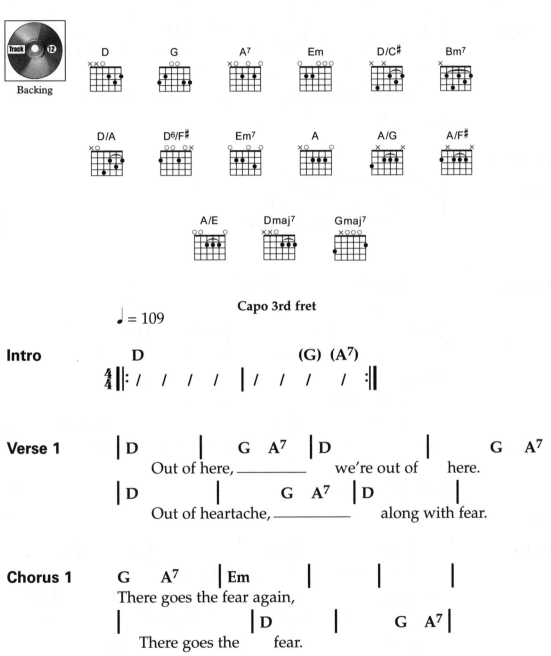

Capo 3rd fret

♩ = 109

Intro   D   (G) (A⁷)

$\frac{4}{4}$ ‖: / / / / | / / / / :‖

Verse 1 |D | G   A⁷ |D | G   A⁷
Out of here, _____ we're out of   here.
|D | G   A⁷ |D |
Out of heartache, _____ along with fear.

Chorus 1   G   A⁷ |Em | | |
There goes the fear again,
| |D | G   A⁷|
There goes the   fear.

Link 1 D   G A⁷

| / / / / | / / / / |

Verse 2 | D | G   A⁷ | D | G   A⁷

And cars speed fast _____ out of   here.

| D | G   A⁷ | D |

And life goes past _____   again so near.

Chorus 2 G   A⁷ | Em | | G

There goes the fear again,   ah _____

| A⁷ | D

There goes the   fear.

Bridge 1 | D/C♯ | Bm⁷

Close your   brown eyes

| D/A | G | D⁶/F♯ | Em |

And lay   down   next to   me.

| Em⁷ | A | A/G

Close your   eyes, _____

| A/F♯ | A/E | Dmaj⁷ |

Lay   down,   'cause there goes the fear.

| A |

Let it go. _____

Middle | Em⁷ | G | D | A

You turn around and life's passed you by.

| Em⁷ | G | D | A

You look to ones you love to ask them why.

| Em⁷ | G | D | A

You look to those you love to justify.

| Em⁷ | G | D

You turn around and life's passed you by,

```
|A              |D          |        (G)  (A⁷)  |
Passed you by again.        /   /   /   /
```

Link 2   D   (G) A⁷
```
| /   /   /   /  | /   /   /   /  |
```

Verse 3
```
|D            |      G  A⁷ |D              |      G  A⁷
And late last night, _____     makes up her mind _____
|D         |     G   A⁷ |D        |
Another fight _____    left behind.
```

Chorus 3
```
G     A⁷     |Em       |          |G
There goes the fear again,    let it go.
|      A⁷         |D       |        G   A⁷  |
There goes the    fear.    /   /   /   /
```

Link 3   D   G A⁷
```
| /   /   /   /  | /   /   /   /  |
```

Bridge 2
```
|D        |D/C♯        |Bm⁷      |A
Close your     brown     eyes _____
         |G                 |D⁶/F♯  |Em
And lay       down         next  to  me.
|Em⁷            |A      |A/G      |A/F♯
Close your     eyes, _____ lay        down
|A/E                    |Dmaj⁷
'Cause there goes the fear
|          |A      |
Let it go.
```

Middle 2

| Em⁷ | G | D | A |

You turn around and life's passed you by. _____

| Em⁷ | G | D | A |

You look to ones you love to ask them why. _____

| Em⁷ | G | D | A |

You look to those you love to justify. _____

| Em⁷ | G | D | A |

You turn around and life's passed you by, _____

Middle 3

| Em⁷ | G |

Think of me when you're coming down

| D | A |

But don't look back when leaving town.

| Em⁷ | G |

Oh, think of me when he's calling out

| D | A |

But don't look back when leaving town.

| Em⁷ | G |

Yeah, think of me when you close your eyes

| D | A |

But don't look back when you break up ties.

| Em⁷ | G |

Think of me when you're coming down

| D | A | D | D/C♯ | Bm⁷ |

But don't look back when leaving town to me.   / / / / / / / /

Chorus 4

| A | G | D⁶/F♯ | Em |

There goes the fear again,   ah. _____

| Em⁷ | A | A/G | A/F♯ |

There goes _____ the   fear,

| A/E | Dmaj⁷ | | A | | |

There goes   the fear,   let it go.

36

Instrumental   Em⁷   Gmaj⁷   D   A

‖: / / / / | / / / / | / / / / | / / / / :‖

Coda

| Em⁷ | G
Ah, think of me when you close your eyes,

| D | A
But don't look back when you break-up ties.

| Em⁷ | G
Think of me when you're coming down

| D | A | Em⁷ | G |
But don't look back when leaving town to me.

D   A   Em⁷   G

| / / / / | / / / / ‖: / / / / | / / / / |

D   A   N.C.

| / / / / | / / / / :‖ 13 bars percussion to end   ‖

37

Silent Sigh

Words and Music by
DAMON GOUGH

Fmaj⁷ C G Am⁷ G/B

♩ = 102

Intro

Fmaj⁷
4/4 | / / / / | / / / / | / / / / | / / / / |

C
| / / / / | / / / / | / / / / | / / / / |

Fmaj⁷
| / / / / | / / / / | / / / / | / / / / |

| C | | | | Fmaj7 | | ‖
Ooh-ah, ooh-ah, ooh-ah, ooh-ah,   ooh. _____

Verse 1

| Fmaj⁷ | | C
     Come see what we all talk about:

People moving to the Moon

Stop, baby, don't go; stop here.
| G   Am⁷ | G/B   G
Never stop living   here   'til it
| Fmaj⁷ |
Eats the   heart from your soul,

Keeps down the sound of

Chorus 1

| C |
Your silent sigh,

| | | Fmaj7
   Silent sigh, silent sigh

|
Silent, silent, silent.

| |
Keeps down all.

| C
Move me down.

| | | |
Could we love each other? _____   oh,

Instrumental 1 Fmaj⁷

| / / / / | / / / / | / / / / | / / / ooh —|

C

| ____ye - | ah / / / | / / / / | / / / / |

Fmaj⁷

| / / / / | / / / / |

Verse 2

| Fmaj⁷ | | C
   Come see what we all talk about:

| |
People moving to the Moon

|
Stop, baby, don't go; stop here.

| G   Am⁷ | G/B   G
Never stop living   here   'til it

| Fmaj⁷ |
Eats the   heart from your soul,

|
Keeps down the sound of

Chorus 2

| C |
Your silent sigh,

| | | Fmaj⁷
   Silent sigh, silent sigh

|
Silent, silent, silent.

| |
Keeps down all.

     | C
Move me down.

|
But don't love each other.

| |
   No, don't love each other.

| G   Am⁷ | G/B   G
Never gonna be the   same,   baby, oh.

| Fmaj⁷ | | |
    See, sigh,   see, sigh,   see, sigh,   sigh ⸻⸻

Coda

| C | | |
Silent sigh,   silent, silent, silent,

| Fmaj⁷ | |
Silent, si - lent, (silent sigh.)

| | C
Please don't we all, move me down.

| | | | Fmaj⁷
(Silent sigh), silent,   silent, silent, silent sigh.

| | | | C
   Silent sigh,   move me down,

| | | |
we're gonna love each other.   / / / /   / / / /

40

(Vocal ad lib.)

Instrumental 2   Fmaj^7

‖: / / / / | / / / / | / / / / | / / / / |

C

| / / / / | / / / / | / / / / | / / / / :‖

Repeat to fade

Silent To The Dark

Track 14
Backing

Words and Music by
TOM WHITE

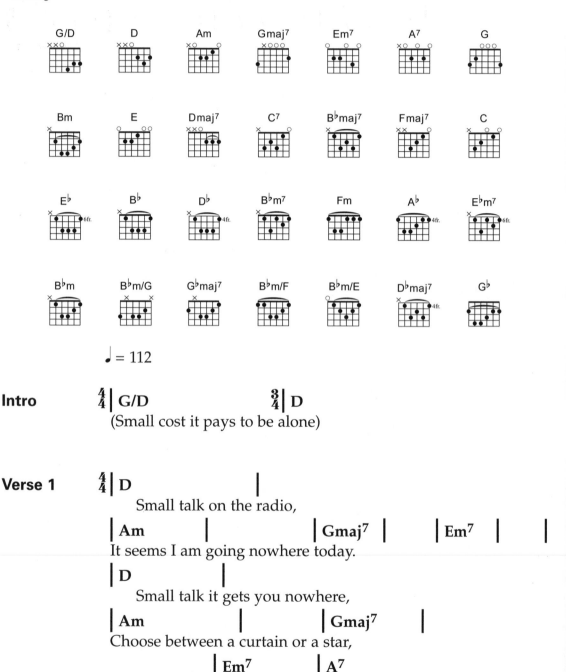

♩ = 112

Intro $\frac{4}{4}$ | G/D $\frac{3}{4}$ | D
(Small cost it pays to be alone)

Verse 1 $\frac{4}{4}$ | D |
    Small talk on the radio,
| Am | | Gmaj⁷ | | Em⁷ | | |
It seems I am going nowhere today.
| D |
    Small talk it gets you nowhere,
| Am | Gmaj⁷ |
Choose between a curtain or a star,
        | Em⁷ | A⁷
And I'm silent to the dark.

Chorus 1

      | D | G

'Cause when I needed someone to talk to,

      | Bm | E

You were the only one around.

| Em^7 | G | D | A^7 |

  A small cost it pays to be alone. / / / /

Verse 2

| D |

  Small talk on the radio

| Am | | Gmaj^7 | | Em^7 | |

It seems I am going nowhere today, not today.

| D |

  Small talk it gets you nowhere,

| Am | | Gmaj^7 |

I'm silent to the dark and tepid

  | Em^7 | A^7

Only when you ask.

Chorus 2

      | D | G

'Cause when I needed someone to talk to,

      | Bm | E

You were the only one around.

| Em^7 | G | Dmaj^7 | A^7 |

  A small cost it pays to be alone. / / / /

      | D | G

And when I needed someone to talk to,

      | Bm | E

You were the only one around.

| Em^7 | G | Dmaj^7 | C^7 | G | A^7 |

  A small cost it pays to be alone.

Link

    Bbmaj^7

   / / / / | / / / / |

Bridge

| Fmaj⁷ |
And you can do anything you want,

| B♭maj⁷ |
And you can do anything you want,

| Fmaj⁷ |
You can do anything you want,

| B♭maj⁷ | | C |
It doesn't mat   -   -   -   ter,

| E♭ | | B♭ |
It doesn't mat   -   -   -   -   ter.

Chorus 3

N.C. | D | G
'Cause when I needed someone to talk to,

| Bm | E
You were the only one around.

| Em⁷ | G | Dmaj⁷ | A⁷ |
A small cost it pays to be alone.   /   /   /   /

| D | G
And when I needed someone to talk to,

| Bm | E
You were the only one around,

| Em⁷ | G | Dmaj⁷ | C⁷ | G | A⁷ |
A small cost it pays to be alone. _____

(freely)

Instrumental 1   D♭   B♭m⁷   D♭   D♭

| /   /   /   / | / ‖ |

Fm   A♭   E♭m⁷

| | | | | |

| B♭m
And when I needed someone.

| B♭m⁷ | B♭m/G | G♭maj⁷ | F |
To talk to,   to talk to,   to talk to.

Instrumental 2 B♭m   B♭m⁷   B♭m/G   G♭maj⁷

‖: / / / / | / / / / | / / / / | / / / / :‖

Play 3 times

♩ = 92

B♭m   B♭m⁷

‖: / / / / | / / / / | / / / / | / / / / |

B♭m/G   G♭maj⁷

| / / / / | / / / / | / / / / | / / / / |

B♭m/F   B♭m/E

| / / / / | / / / / | / / / / | / / / / |

E♭m⁷   D♭   Db maj⁷

| / / / / | / / / / | / / / / | / / / / :‖

Play 3 times

B♭m   B♭m⁷

| / / / / | / / / / | / / / / | / / / / |

B♭m/G   G♭maj⁷

| / / / / | / / / / | / / / / |

Chorus 4 | D♭ | G♭

'Cause when I needed someone to talk to,

                    | B♭m | E♭

You were the only one around.

| E♭m⁷ | G♭ | D♭   ‖

       A small cost it pays to be alone.

45

Tender

Words and Music by
DAMON ALBARN, ALEX JAMES,
GRAHAM COXON AND DAVID ROWNTREE

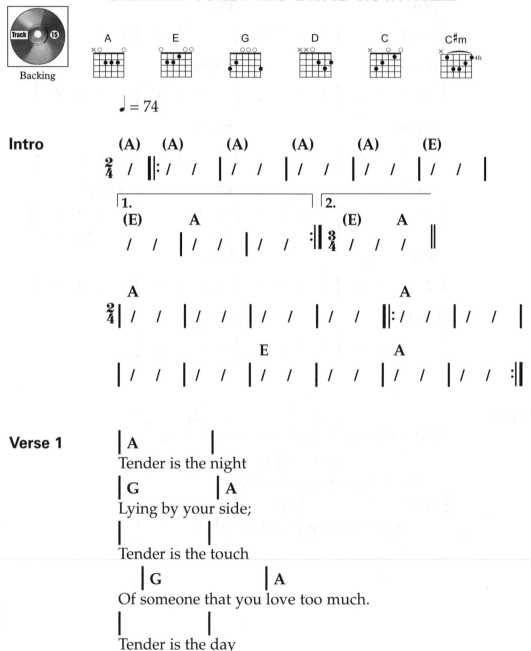

Verse 1

|A |
Tender is the night

|G |A
Lying by your side;

| |
Tender is the touch

          |G |A
Of someone that you love too much.

| |
Tender is the day

```
|G          |A
The demons go away.

|           |
Lord,  I need to find
|G                 |A
Someone who can heal my mind.
```

Chorus 1   ‖: A |
```
        Come on, come on, come on,
|D     |C
     Get through it.
|A                      |
        Come on, come on, come on,
|C♯m              |D              :‖
        Love's the greatest thing
|C♯m         |D
     That we have.
     |C♯m            |D
I'm waiting for that feeling,
        |C♯m             |D
I'm waiting for that feeling,
|A               |G       |A            |
Waiting for that feeling to      come. _____
```

Bridge 1 |A |
```
Oh my baby,

              |            |
Oh my baby,

        |E
Oh why?

|        |A     |
Oh    my.

        |            |
Oh my baby,
```

|A |
Oh my baby,
　　|E
Oh why?
| |A | |
Oh   my.

Verse 2　　|A |
Tender is the ghost
　　|G |A
The ghost I love the most.
| |
Hiding from the sun
|G |A
Waiting for the night to come.
| |
Tender is my heart
　　|G |A
For screwing up my life.
| |
Lord, I need to find
|G |A
Someone who can heal my mind.

Chorus 2　　‖: A |
Come on, come on, come on,
|D |C
Get through it.
|A |
Come on, come on, come on,
|C♯m |D   :‖
Love's the greatest thing
|C♯m |D
That we have.

```
        |C#m          |D
I'm waiting for that feeling,
        |C#m          |D
I'm waiting for that feeling,
 |A                |G      |A            |
 Waiting for that feeling to   come. _____
```

Bridge 2
```
                |A        |
Oh my baby,

              |          |
Oh my baby,
              |E
Oh why?
 |     |A      |
Oh    my.

              |          |
Oh my baby,

              |          |
Oh my baby,
              |E
Oh why?
 |     |A    |      |
Oh    my.
```

Guitar solo
```
     A              G      A                    G      A
 | / / | / / | / / | / / | / / | / / | / / | / / ‖
```

Chorus 3
```
 ‖: A                |
      Come on, come on, come on,
 |D      |C
      Get through it.
 |A                  |
      Come on, come on, come on,
```

49

```
| C♯m          | D            :‖
        Love's the greatest thing
| C♯m      | D
        That we have.
        | C♯m          | D
I'm waiting for that feeling,
        | C♯m          | D
I'm waiting for that feeling,
| A            | G        | A            |
Waiting for that feeling to    come. _____
```

Bridge 3
```
                | A        |
        Oh my baby,

                |         |
        Oh my baby,
                | E
        Oh why?
        |    | A    |
        Oh   my.

                |         |
        Oh my baby,

                |         |
        Oh my baby,
                | E
        Oh why?
        |    | A    |    |
        Oh   my.
```

Verse 3
```
        | A        |
        Tender is the night
        | G        | A
        Lying by your side;
        |         |
        Tender is the touch
```

|G |A

Of someone that you love too much.

| |

Tender is my heart, you know,

|G |A

For screwing up my life.

| |

Oh Lord, I need to find

|G |A

Someone who can heal my mind.

Chorus 4   ‖: A |

Come on, come on, come on,

|D |C

Get through it.

|A |

Come on, come on, come on,

|C♯m |D   :‖

Love's the greatest thing

|C♯m |D

That we have.

|C♯m |D

I'm waiting for that feeling,

|C♯m |D

I'm waiting for that feeling,

|A |G |A |

Waiting for that feeling to   come.

Bridge 4 |A |

Oh my baby,

| |

Oh my baby,

|E

Oh why?

| | |A | |
Oh   my.

| |
Oh my baby,

| |
Oh my baby,

|E
Oh why?

| |A | |
Oh   my.

Bridge 5

|A |
Oh my baby,

| |
Oh my baby,

|E
Oh why?

| |A |
Oh   my.

| |
Oh my baby,

| |
Oh my baby,

|E
Oh why?

| |A | |
Oh   my.

(with vocal ad libs)

Bridge 6

|A |
Oh my baby,

| |
Oh my baby,

|E
Oh why?

| | A | |
Oh   my.

| | | |
Oh my baby,

| A | |
Oh my baby,

| E
Oh why?

| | A | | || *to fade*
Oh   my.

Underdog
(Save Me)

Words and Music by
OLLY KNIGHTS AND GALE PARIDJANIAN

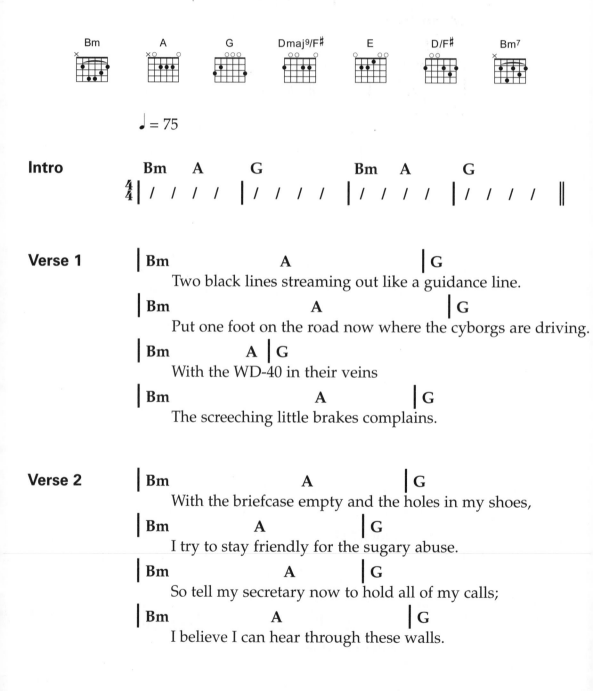

| Bm | A | G | Dmaj9/F# | E | D/F# | Bm7 |

♩ = 75

Intro

Bm A G   Bm A G

4/4 | / / / / | / / / / | / / / / | / / / / ‖

Verse 1

| Bm   A | G
Two black lines streaming out like a guidance line.

| Bm   A | G
Put one foot on the road now where the cyborgs are driving.

| Bm   A | G
With the WD-40 in their veins

| Bm   A | G
The screeching little brakes complains.

Verse 2

| Bm   A | G
With the briefcase empty and the holes in my shoes,

| Bm   A | G
I try to stay friendly for the sugary abuse.

| Bm   A | G
So tell my secretary now to hold all of my calls;

| Bm   A | G
I believe I can hear through these walls.

Chorus 1

|A   Dmaj^9/F$^\sharp$ |G   E
Oh please save me,   save me from myself.

|A Dmaj^9/F$^\sharp$ |G   E
I can't be   the only one stuck on the shelf.

|A   Dmaj^9/F$^\sharp$
You said you'd always _____

|G   E |A Dmaj^9/F$^\sharp$ $\frac{2}{4}$|G D/F$^\sharp$ $\frac{4}{4}$|E |
Fall for the under - dog.   /   /   / / / /

Link

   Bm   A   G   Bm   A   G

| / / / / | / / / / | / / / / | / / / / |

Verse 3

|Bm   A |G
Well, I've been dreaming of jet-streams and kicking up dust,

|Bm   A |G
A thirty-seven thousand foot wanderlust.

|Bm   A |G
And with skyline number nine ticked off in my mind

|Bm   A
Can you hear me screaming out now

     |G
Through the telephone lines?

Chorus 2

|A   Dmaj^9/F$^\sharp$ |G   E
Oh please save me,   save me from myself.

|A Dmaj^9/F$^\sharp$ |G   E
I can't be   the only one stuck on the shelf.

|A   Dmaj^9/F$^\sharp$
You said you'd always _____

|G   E |A Dmaj^9/F$^\sharp$ $\frac{2}{4}$|G D/F$^\sharp$ $\frac{4}{4}$|E |
Fall for the under - dog.   /   /   / / / /

Guitar solo Bm A G   Bm A G

$\|:$ / / / / | / / / / | / / / / | / / / / :$\|$

Coda

Play 3 times

$\|:$ A   Dmaj^9/F$^\sharp$ | G   E   :$\|$ A   Dmaj^9/F$^\sharp$

Save   me.   Save   me.

G D/F$^\sharp$ E   Bm^7

$\frac{2}{4}$| /   / $\frac{4}{4}$| /   /   /   / | / $\|$

All You Good Good People

Words and Music by
DANIEL McNAMARA AND RICHARD McNAMARA

Verse 1

I feel like I meant something,
you always say you need more time.
Well, I'll stay right here and I'll wait for good
Until I find a love worth mine.
Some day you've got it coming,
it hurts me when I read the sign
So loud and clear that I'll make you glad
If I'm leaving first and crying.

Chorus 1

All you good, good people listen to me:
You're just about done with the way that you feel.
There's nothing rings home enough to dig your heels in.
You don't have to leave me to see what I mean.
All you good, good people listen to me.

Bridge

And all I wanna do is find my name upon the line
Before I have to lose this I want time.

Chorus 2

All you good, good people listen to me:
You're just about done with the way that you feel.
Nothing rings home enough to dig your heels in.
You don't have to leave me to see what I mean.
Lose all your fears – they are keeping you down.
You won't have to fake it while I'm around.
All you good, good people listen to me.

Coda

Listen to me,
Listen to me,
Listen to me.

American English

Words and Music by
COLIN NEWTON, RODDY WOOMBLE,
ROD PRYCE-JONES AND BOB FAIRFOULL

Verse 1

Songs, when the truth are all dedicated to you.
In this invisible world I choose to live in.
And if you believe that then now I understand why words mean so much to you.
They'll never be about you.

Verse 2

Maybe you're young without youth,
Or maybe you're old without knowing anything's true.
I think you're young without youth.

Pre-Chorus

Then you contract the American dream, you never look up once.
You've contracted American dreams.
I require you to stop and look up.

Chorus

Sing a song about myself, keep singing a song about myself.
Not some invisible world.

Verse 3

Constantly searching to find something new,
But what will you find when you think that nothing's true?
Maybe it's that nothing is new.
So you let me hear songs that were written all about you.
The good songs weren't written for you.
They'll never be about you.

Pre-Chorus

And you contract the American dream, you never look up once.
You've contracted American dreams,
You'll never look up once, so don't look up.

Chorus

Sing a song about myself, keep singing a song about myself.
Not some invisible world.
Sing a song about myself, keep singing a song about myself.
Not some invisible world.

Bridge

And I won't tell you what this means, 'cos you already know.
And I won't tell you what this means, 'cos you already know.

Chorus

So sing a song about myself, keep singing a song about myself.
Not some invisible world.
And you came along and found the weak heart that you've always wanted.
And let yourself be everything that you've always wanted.
It doesn't have to be so decided that you've always wanted.
And no need for explanations you've always wanted.

Outro

And you'll find what you find when you find there's nothing.
And you'll find what you find when you find there's nothing.

The Drugs Don't Work

Words and Music by
RICHARD ASHCROFT

Pre Verse 1

All this talk of getting old, it's getting me down my love.
Like a cat in a bag waiting to drown, this time I'm coming down.

Verse 1

And I hope you're thinking of me as you lay down on your side.
Now the drugs don't work they just make you worse
But I know I'll see your face again.

Chorus 1

Now the drugs don't work they just make you worse
But I know I'll see your face again.

Verse 2

But I know I'm on a losing streak, as I pass down my old street.
And if you want to show just let me know and I'll sing in your ear again.

Chorus 2

Now the drugs don't work they just make you worse
But I know I'll see your face again.

Bridge 1

Coz baby ooh, if heaven calls I'm coming too.
Just like you say, you'll leave my life, I'm better off dead.

Verse 3

All this talk of getting old, it's getting me down my love.
Like a cat in a bag waiting to drown, this time I'm coming down.

Chorus 3

Now the drugs don't work they just make you worse
But I know I'll see your face again.

Bridge 2

Coz baby ooh, if heaven calls I'm coming too.
Just like you say, you'll leave my life, I'm better off dead.
But if you want to show, then just let me know
And I'll sing in your ear again.

Chorus 4

Now the drugs don't work they just make you worse
But I know I'll see your face again,
Yeah I know I'll see your face again,
Yeah I know I'll see your face...

Grace

Words and Music by
DANIEL GOFFEY, GARETH COOMBES,
MICHAEL QUINN AND ROBERT COOMBES

Verse 1

Well we jumped all night on your trampoline.
When you kissed the sky it made your sister scream,
You ate our chips, and you drank our coke.
And then you showed me Mars through your telescope.

Chorus 1

Oh Grace. Save your money for the children.
Oh Grace. Save your money for the children.
Oh Grace. Save your money for the children.
Oh Grace. Save your money, save your money. Go!

Verse 2

Well you sang your songs and you made us laugh.
So we captured you in a photograph,
And when the star came out, your mother called your name,
But when the morning comes, we'll be together again.

Chorus 1

Oh Grace. Save your money for the children.
Oh Grace. Save your money for the children.
Oh Grace. Save your money for the children.
Oh Grace. Save your money, save your money. Go!

Bridge

Save your money.
Save your money for the...
Save your money for the children.
Save your money for the children.

Chorus 1

Oh Grace. Save your money for the children.
Oh Grace. Save your money, save your money. Go!

Handbags And Gladrags

Words and Music by
MIKE D'ABO

Verse 1

Ever see a blind man cross the road tryin' to make the other side?
Ever see a young girl growing old tryin' to make herself a bride?

Chorus

So what becomes of you, my love?
When they have finally stripped you of the handbags and gladrags
That your poor old grand-dad had to sweat to buy you.

Verse 2

Once I was a young man and all I thought I had to do was smile.
Well you are still a young girl and you bought everything in style.

Chorus

So once you think you're in, you're out
'Cos you don't mean a single thing without the handbags and the gladrags
That your poor old grand-dad had to sweat to buy you.

Verse 3

Sing a song of sixpence for his sake and drink a bottle full of rye.
Sour and twenty blackbirds in a cake. And bake them all in a pie.

Chorus

They told me you missed school today
So what I suggest, you just throw them all away. The handbags and the gladrags
That your poor old grand-dad had to sweat to buy you.

Chorus

They told me you missed school today
So what I suggest, you just throw them all away. The handbags and the gladrags
That your poor old grand-dad had to sweat to buy you.

Hotel Yorba

Words and Music by
JACK WHITE

Verse 1

I was watching with one eye on the other side,
I had 15 people telling me to move, I got moving on my mind.
I found shelter in some thoughts turning wheels around.
I said thirty-nine times that I love you to the beauty I have found.

Chorus 1

Well, it's one, two, three, four, take the elevator
At the Hotel Yorba, I'll be glad to see ya later
All they got inside is vacancy.

Verse 2

I've been thinking of a little place down by the lake:
They got a dirty, old road leading up to the house
I wonder how long it will take 'til we're alone?
Sitting on the front porch of that home,
Stomping our feet on the wooden boards;
We never got to worry about locking the door.

Chorus 2

Well, it's one, two, three, four, take the elevator
At the Hotel Yorba, I'll be glad to see ya later
All they got inside is vacancy.

Verse 3

It might sound silly for me to think childish thoughts like these
But I'm so tired of acting tough and I'm gonna do what I please.
Let's get married in a big cathedral by a priest,
'Cause if I'm the man that you love the most you can say 'I do' at least.

Chorus 3

Well, it's one, two, three, four, take the elevator
At the Hotel Yorba, I'll be glad to see ya later
All they got inside is vacancy.

Chorus 4

And it's four, five, six, seven, grab your umbrella,
Grab a hold of me 'cause I'm your favourite fella,
All they got inside is vacancy.

Karma Police

Words and Music by
THOMAS YORKE, JONATHAN GREENWOOD,
PHILIP SELWAY, COLIN GREENWOOD
AND EDWARD O'BRIEN

Verse 1

Karma police, arrest this man he talks in maths
He buzzes like a fridge
He's like a detuned radio.

Verse 2

Karma police, arrest this girl
Her Hitler hairdo is making me feel ill
And we have crashed her party.

Bridge 1

This is what you get
This is what you get
This is what you get when you mess with us.

Verse 3

Karma police, I've given all I can
It's not enough I've given all I can
But we're still on the payroll.

Bridge 2

This is what you get
This is what you get
This is what you get when you mess with us.

Outro

And for a minute there, I lost myself, I lost myself
And for a minute there, I lost myself, I lost myself.
For a minute there, I lost myself, I lost myself
Phew, for a minute there, I lost myself, I lost myself

Love Burns

Words and Music by
PETER HAYES, ROBERT BEEN
AND **NICHOLAS JAGO**

Verse 1

Never thought I'd see her go away,
She learned I loved her today.
Never thought I'd see her cry,
And I learned how to love her today.
Never thought I'd rather die
Than try to keep her by my side.

Chorus 1

Now she's gone love burns inside me.

Verse 2

Nothing else can hurt us now,
No loss, our love's been hung on a cross.
Nothing seems to make a sound,
And now it's all so clear somehow.
Nothing really matters now,
We're gone and on our way.

Chorus 2

Now she's gone love burns inside me.

Bridge

She cuts my skin and bruise my lips,
She's everything to me.
She tears my clothes and burns my eyes,
She's all I want to see.
She brings the cold and scars my soul,
She's heaven sent to me.

Chorus 3

Now she's gone love burns inside me.

Coda

Never thought I'd need you like the way that I do, yeah.
With a kiss, my love, and a wish you're gone.
With a kiss, my love, and a wish you're gone.
Never thought I'd need you like the way that I do.
With a kiss, my love, and a wish you're gone.
With a kiss, my love, and a wish you're gone.

Chorus 4

Now she's gone love burns inside me.

Poor Misguided Fool

Words and Music by
JAMES WALSH, JAMES STELFOX,
BARRY WESTHEAD AND **BENJAMIN BYRNE**

Verse 1

Soon as you sound like him, give me a call.
When you're so sensitive, it's a long way to fall.
Whenever you need a home, I will be there.
Whenever you're all alone, and nobody cares.

Chorus 1

You're just a poor misguided fool
Who thinks they know what I should do.
Life for me and life for you.
I lose my right to a point of view.

Verse 2

Whenever you reach for me, I'll be your guide.
Whenever you need someone so keep it inside.
Whenever you need a home, I will be there.
Whenever you're all alone, and nobody cares.

Chorus 2

You're just a poor misguided fool
Who thinks they know what I should do.
Life for me and life for you.
I lose my right to a point of view.

Bridge

I'll be your guide in the morning.
You'll cover up bullet-holes.

Verse 3

Soon as you sound like him, give me a call.
When you're so sensitive, it's a long way to fall.

Chorus 3

You're just a poor misguided fool
Who thinks they know what I should do.
Life for me and life for you.
I lose my right to a point of view.

Powder Blue

Words and Music by
GUY GARVEY, MARK POTTER, CRAIG POTTER,
RICHARD JUPP AND PETE TURNER

Verse 1

Your eyes are just like black spiders,
Your hair and dress in ribbons. Babycakes.
In despair or incoherent, nothing inbetween.
China white, my bride tonight smiling on the tiles.

Chorus 1

Bring that minute back
We never get so close as when the sunward flight begins.
I share it all with you powder blue.

Verse 2

Stumble through the crowds together.
They're trying to ignore us – that's okay.
I'm proud to be the one you hold when the shakes begin
Sallow-skinned, starry-eyed, blessed in our skin.

Chorus 2

Bring that minute back
We never get so close to death. Makes you so alive.
I share it all with you, powder blue. Hey, yeah.

Chorus 3

Bring that minute back
We never get so close as when the sunward flight begins.
I share it all with you powder blue.

There Goes The Fear

Words and Music by
JIMI GOODWIN, JEZ WILLIAMS AND **ANDY WILLIAMS**

Verse 1

Out of here, we're out of here.
Out of heartache, along with fear.

Chorus 1

There goes the fear again, there goes the fear.

Verse 2

And cars speed fast out of here.
And life goes past again so near.

Chorus 2

There goes the fear again, ah there goes the fear.

Bridge 1

Close your brown eyes and lay down next to me.
Close your eyes, lay down,
'cause there goes the fear. Let it go.

Middle 1

You turn around and life's passed you by.
You look to ones you love to ask you why.
You look to those you love to justify.
You turn around and life's passed you by, passed you by again.

Verse 3

And late last night, makes up her mind
Another fight left behind.

Chorus 3

There goes the fear again, let it go. There goes the fear.

Bridge 2

Close your brown eyes and lay down next to me.
Close your eyes, lay down,
'cause there goes the fear. Let it go.

Middle 2

You turn around and life's passed you by.
You look to ones you love to ask you why.
You look to those you love to justify.
You turn around and life's passed you by,

Middle 3

Think of me when you're coming down
But don't look back when leaving town.
Oh, think of me when he's calling out
But don't look back when leaving town.
Yeah, think of me when you close your eyes
But don't look back when you break up ties.
Think of me when you're coming down
But don't look back when leaving town to me.

Chorus 4

There goes the fear again, ah.
There goes the fear, there goes the fear, let it go.

Coda

Ah, think of me when you close your eyes,
But don't look back when you break up ties.
Think of me when you're coming down
But don't look back when leaving town to me.

Silent Sigh

Words and Music by
DAMON GOUGH

Verse 1

Come see what we talk about: People moving to the moon
Stop, baby, don't go; stop here.
Never stop living here 'til it eats the heart from your soul,
Keeps down the sound of

Chorus 1

Your silent sigh,
SIlent sigh, silent sigh silent, silent, silent.
Keeps down all. Move me down. Could we love each other?

Verse 2

Come see what we talk about: People moving to the moon
Stop, baby, don't go; stop here.
Never stop living here 'til it eats the heart from your soul,
Keeps down the sound of

Chorus 2

Your silent sigh,
SIlent sigh, silent sigh silent, silent, silent.
Keeps down all. Move me down. But don't love each other.
No, don't love each other.
Never gonna be the same, baby, oh.
See, sigh, see, sigh, see, sigh, sigh

Coda

Silent sigh, silent, silent, silent,
Silent, silent, (silent sigh.)
Please don't we all, move me down.
(Silent sigh), silent, silent, silent, silent sigh.
Silent sigh, move me down,
We're gonna love each other.

Silent To The Dark

Words and Music by
TOM WHITE

Verse 1

Small talk on the radio, it seems I am going nowhere today.
Small talk it gets you nowhere, choose between a curtain or a star,
And I'm silent to the dark.

Chorus 1

'cause when I needed someone to talk to, you were the only one around.
A small cost it pays to be alone.

Verse 2

Small talk on the radio, it seems I am going nowhere today, not today.
Small talk it gets you nowhere,
I'm silent to the dark and tepid only when you ask.

Chorus 2

'cause when I needed someone to talk to, you were the only one around.
A small cost it pays to be alone.
'cause when I needed someone to talk to, you were the only one around.
A small cost it pays to be alone.

Bridge

And you can do anything you want, and you can do anything you want,
You can do anything you want, it doesn't matter, it doesn't matter.

Chorus 3

'cause when I needed someone to talk to, you were the only one around.
A small cost it pays to be alone.
'cause when I needed someone to talk to, you were the only one around.
A small cost it pays to be alone.

And when I needed someone.
To talk to, to talk to, to talk to.

Chorus 4

'cause when I needed someone to talk to, you were the only one around.
A small cost it pays to be alone.

Tender

Words and Music by
DAMON ALBARN, ALEX JAMES,
GRAHAM COXON AND DAVID ROWNTREE

Verse 1

Tender is the night, lying by your side;
Tender is the touch of someone that you love too much.
Tender is the day the demons go away.
Lord, I need to find someone who can heal my mind.

Chorus 1

Come one, come on, come on, get through it.
Come one, come on, come on, love's the greatest thing that we have.
I'm waiting for that feeling, I'm waiting for that feeling,
Waiting for that feeling to come.

Bridge 1

Oh my baby, oh my baby, oh why? Oh my.
Oh my baby, oh my baby, oh why? Oh my.

Verse 2

Tender is the ghost the ghost I love the most.
Hiding from the sun waiting for the night to come.
Tender is my heart for screwing up my life.
Lord, I need to find someone who can heal my mind.

Chorus 2

Come one, come on, come on, get through it.
Come one, come on, come on, love's the greatest thing that we have.
I'm waiting for that feeling, I'm waiting for that feeling,
Waiting for that feeling to come.

Bridge 2

Oh my baby, oh my baby, oh why? Oh my.
Oh my baby, oh my baby, oh why? Oh my.

Chorus 3

Come one, come on, come on, get through it.
Come one, come on, come on, love's the greatest thing that we have.
I'm waiting for that feeling, I'm waiting for that feeling,
Waiting for that feeling to come.

Bridge 3

Oh my baby, oh my baby, oh why? Oh my.
Oh my baby, oh my baby, oh why? Oh my.

Verse 3

Tender is the night, lying by your side;
Tender is the touch of someone that you love too much.
Tender is my heart, you know, for screwing up my life.
Oh Lord, I need to find someone who can heal my mind.

Chorus 4   Come one, come on, come on, get through it.
Come one, come on, come on, love's the greatest thing that we have.
I'm waiting for that feeling, I'm waiting for that feeling,
Waiting for that feeling to come.

Bridge 4   Oh my baby, oh my baby, oh why? Oh my.
Oh my baby, oh my baby, oh why? Oh my.

Bridge 5   Oh my baby, oh my baby, oh why? Oh my.
Oh my baby, oh my baby, oh why? Oh my.

Bridge 6   Oh my baby, oh my baby, oh why? Oh my.
Oh my baby, oh my baby, oh why? Oh my.

Underdog
(Save Me)

Words and Music by
OLLY KNIGHTS AND GALE PARIDJANIAN

Verse 1

Two black lines streaming out like a guidance line.
Put one foot on the road now where the cyborgs are driving.
With the WD-40 in their veins
The screeching little brakes complains.

Verse 2

With the briefcase empty and the holes in my shoes,
I try to stay friendly for the sugary abuse.
So tell my secretary now to hold all of my calls;
I believe I can hear through these walls.

Chorus 1

Oh please save me, save me from myself.
I can't be the only one stuck on the shelf.
You said you'd always fall for the underdog.

Verse 3

Well, I've been dreaming of jet-streams and kicking up dust,
A thirty-seven thousand foot wanderlust.
And with skyline number nine ticked off in my mind
Can you hear me screaming out now through the telephone lines?

Chorus 2

Oh please save me, save me from myself.
I can't be the only one stuck on the shelf.
You said you'd always fall for the underdog.

Coda

Save me. Save me.